MW01105867

This book is dedicated to my Sister

Ruth Ann

Thank you for your love and helping me fulfill my dreams!

I Love You

Nanette

To The Weyand,
Grandchildren,

Reading is fun!
Love,
Nanette
2017

Little Red

Written by Nanette

Illustrations by Pat Thompson

Edited by Ruth H. and Stephanie Taylor

Library of Congress Control Number 2003093990
ISBN 0-9741269-1-8
Published by St. Bernard Publishing
P.O. Box 2218 ♥ Bay City, MI 48707-2218 ♥ 989-892-1348

One bright and sunny day a Daddy Cow and Mama Cow were grazing in a field of clover. They were waiting for the birth of their first baby. Daddy was very big and all black except for a spot of white on his forehead. Mama was smaller with black and white all over except for a big spot of **red** on her forehead.

Both Daddy and Mama cow were very excited about the birth of their new baby and sensed that it was going to be a wonderful surprise. Just as the sun was going down the little calf decided it was time to come into this world. Within five minutes the baby was lying in the clover looking up at her Mama and Daddy.

Mama smiled and said, "Hi **Little Red**. I'm your Mama."

Then Daddy said, "Hi **Little Red**. I'm your Daddy."

The little calf thought "**Little Red**" must be her name and decided to say hello back to them. "Hi Mama and Daddy. I am **Little Red**!"

Her parents laughed so hard they almost fell over.

Little Red wasn't very graceful when she tried to stand. After a couple of tries, she was up on all four legs and wobbled to her Mama and Daddy. They nuzzled **Little Red** and told her they loved her.

8

Little Red ate three times a day and even had a snack before bedtime. She was getting bigger and stronger every day. She walked around the farm by herself to say hello to all the animals. But the more she walked, the more she was aware that the animals were laughing at her. **Little Red** didn't know what was so funny. She didn't think it was very nice to laugh at anyone and they were beginning to hurt her feelings.

10

Little Red decided to ask her parents why all the animals were laughing.

"Mama! Daddy! Where are you? I need to talk to you!" yelled **Little Red**. She had not wandered too far from Mama and Daddy, but she could not see either one of them. She was getting scared!

"Mama! Daddy! Can you hear me?" cried **Little Red**.

"Here we are, **Little Red**. What is the matter?" asked Mama.

"Mama, everyone laughs at me when I say hello to them. Is there something wrong with me?" asked **Little Red**.

"No, **Little Red**. There is nothing wrong with you. You are just different and your difference is what makes you special," said Mama.

"Special? Why am I special?" asked **Little Red**.
Mama knew it was time to tell **Little Red** the story about her grandparents and said, "Your Grandma and Grandpa each had a big **red** spot on their foreheads just like mine. They were told and believed that one day a special cow would be born - a **RED AND WHITE COW** - YOU!"

"Does a **RED AND WHITE** cow get to have friends? Am I ever going to have any friends?" asked **Little Red**. "Everyone has them but me." Mama and Daddy looked at each other, smiled and said, "Yes, **Little Red**. You will have many friends and tomorrow we will show you."

The next day Mama and Daddy took **Little Red** over the hill to meet their neighbor, Granny. Granny was a very special person and had a very special farm. She told **Little Red** that everyone on Granny's Farm had to be kind, always share, help each other, do chores and most of all have lots and lots of fun.

Granny took **Little Red** all around the farm to meet the other animals. **Little Red** waited to see if anyone would laugh at her. To her surprise, no one did. Everyone was very nice.

Little Red even got to meet Granny's neighbor, Dr. Kaydee. He was a veterinarian and took care of all the animals when they didn't feel well.

23

Granny's Farm

24

"Hi **Little Red**!" said Dr. Kaydee. "It is very nice to meet you."

"Hi Dr. Kaydee!" said **Little Red**. "Do you really take care of all the animals on Granny's farm when they are sick?

"Yes **Little Red**. I take care of every animal all over the county," answered Dr. Kaydee. "Are you feeling okay?"

"Oh yes! I feel great!" answered **Little Red**.

"That's good!" said Dr. Kaydee "I'll see you later, I have to go now, take care."

"Goodbye, it was nice to meet you, too!" said **Little Red**.

Later that day, after everyone was done playing, **Little Red** looked at Granny and said, "Gee, my Mama and Daddy were right. It sure is fun to visit your farm and meet all these nice friends. Do you think I can come over and play again sometime soon?"

Granny thought it was a great idea and even asked **Little Red's** Mama and Daddy if they would let **Little Red** stay for the whole summer.

"Please! Please! Please!" pleaded **Little Red**.

"Well of course you can stay for the summer," said Daddy.

"Yippee!" cried **Little Red**. Her parents were thrilled to see **Little Red** so happy.

"Granny, we believe you have a new summer guest," said Mama.

Little Red was very excited!

Throughout the summer, Granny and **Little Red** became very close as they laughed and talked about many things and read wonderful stories. Sometimes Granny even made up her own stories, which was really exciting to everyone on the farm.

One day, while walking around the farm, **Little Red** suddenly shouted out "Granny, there is something **BLUE** near the tree! What is that? Is it an animal? Is it hurt?"

Visit Granny and all her friends on her website!
www.lifeongrannysfarm.com